Radical Sports

SNOWBOARDING

Andy Fraser • • • • • • • • • • • •

Heinemann Library
Chicago, Illinois

Customer Service 888-454-2279

Designed by Celia Floyd
Illustrations by Jeff Edwards
Originated by HBM Print Ltd, Singapore
Printed in Hong Kong by Wing King Tong

04 03 02 01 00
10 9 8 7 6 5 4 3 2 1

Library of Congress Cataloging-in-Publication Data
Fraser, Andy, 1973-
    Snowboarding / Andy Fraser.
      p. cm. – (Radical sports)
    Includes bibliographical references (p.) and index.
    Summary: Introduces the sport of snowboarding, giving a brief history of the sport and discussing the equipment, basic skills, snowboarding events, and places to enjoy the sport.
      ISBN 1-57572-946-6
      1. Snowboarding Juvenile literature. [1. Snowboarding.]
    I. Title. II. Series.
    GV857.S57F73 2000
    796.9—dc21   99-31775
                                                              CIP

Acknowledgments
The Publishers would like to thank the following for permission to reproduce photographs:

K2, p. 4; Burton Snowboards, pp. 5, 6, 8, 9 top, 11 (helmet, hat, and socks), 23; CHOD, courtesy of Whitelines Magazine, p. 7; Steven King, pp. 9 bottom, 10-19; Stockfile/Stephen Behr, pp. 20, 25; Burton Snowboards/Scott Needham, p. 21; Snowboard Klinik, p. 22; Nick Hamilton, courtesy of Whitelines Magazine, pp. 24, 28, 29; Allsport/Shaun Botterill, p. 26; Allsport/Brian Bahr, p. 27.

Cover photograph reproduced with permission of Whitelines.

Our thanks to Ben DiMaggio for his comments in the preparation of this book. Thanks also to Anna Lawlor, Hamish Duncan, James and Thomas Reynolds, and Sam Walker, who kindly appeared in the technique photographs. Thanks to Gary Baker, Mark Chesterfield, and all the staff at the Tamworth Snowdome.

Every effort has been made to contact copyright holders of any material reproduced in this book. Any omissions will be rectified in subsequent printings if notice is given to the Publisher.

Any words appearing in the text in bold, **like this**, are explained in the Glossary.

CONTENTS

INTRODUCTION

A short history

Snowboarding is the ultimate sporting success story. In just 30 years it has grown from nothing into an official Olympic event practiced by millions. The secret of its success is simple—snowboarding is great fun.

How it started

The origins of snowboarding lie in skateboarding and surfing. The sport was developed by enthusiasts who wanted to transport the thrill of skate parks or riding waves to the mountains.

The earliest snowboard was called the Snurfer. It was invented in the mid-1960s by an American surfer named Sherman Poppen. It had a primitive design and looked a bit like a water ski without **bindings**. The rider held a rope attached to the front of the board for balance and enjoyed a frightening ride down the slope.

There is no limit to the fun you can have snowboarding. If you practice hard, soon you too will be enjoying the thrill of flying through the air.

Snowboard pioneer Jake Burton models one of his boards. The sport he helped invent is now one of the fastest-growing in the world.

Special developments

In the 1970s the idea was taken a step further by such pioneers as American Jake Burton and the U.S. skateboard champion, Tom Sims. Bindings to attach the feet to the board were added, and the boards were made lighter and more responsive.

In the early days snowboarders were not welcomed by skiers. They were even prevented from riding **ski lifts** or banned from resorts altogether. But over the years the sport has become more accepted, and skiers and boarders now share the slopes.

Today's sport

Snowboarding continues to grow and evolve. Each season, new events and technical developments raise it to an even more advanced level. The number of riders jumping aboard continues to increase, and nearly half of all boarders are between the ages of six and seventeen. So don't get left behind—get boarding!

THE BOARD

The right board for you

To enjoy snowboarding, you need the right kind of board. They may look similar, but they don't all perform in the same way. Remember, there is more to a snowboard than just a colorful design.

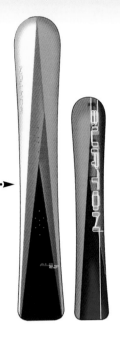

The alpine board ·····································

The **alpine** board is designed for speed. It is narrow, with a curved **nose** and flat **tail**. It is stiff for stability at high speeds and its long edges help it **carve** through the snow. Experts use alpine boards for **slalom** races so they can make fast, precise turns as they zigzag between gates.

·········· *The freestyle board*

This board is for jumping and tricks. It is shorter and fatter than the alpine version. It is called a **twin-tip** because it is the same at both ends, which means you can spin it around and travel backwards. **Freestyle** boards are used for competitions like the **halfpipe**.

·········· *The freeride board*

The **freeride** is for all types of terrain. It is long enough for neat turns but still flexible enough for tricks. If you would like to try a bit of everything instead of specializing, this is the one for you.

BOARD TIPS

Choose a board that fits you. If you have big feet and a narrow board, your heels will drag in the snow as you turn. If you have small feet and the board is too wide, turning will be difficult. The heavier or taller you are, the longer the board you will need. Always ask for advice.

Board design

The snowboard is a sandwich of different layers. The inner core is made of wood, foam, or aluminum. This is strengthened with a covering of fiberglass strands. The logo and design are laid on top and sealed with a transparent top coat. The underside is covered with a clear material called **P-tex**, which helps the board glide smoothly. The board's edges are made of hardened steel and must be sharp for turning.

Logo and design with a transparent topcoat ⸺

Fiberglass covering ⸺

Inner core ⸺

Steel board edge ⸺

Fiberglass covering ⸺

P-tex coat ⸺

LEASHES

 Leashes are not just for dogs. Snowboards have no brakes—if you leave them on a slope they will speed off, endangering other skiers and boarders. When you put the board on, attach the leash to your boot or leg before you do anything else.

Turning and jumping put boards under intense pressure, so they have to be tough. This rider is pushing his freestyle board to the limit in the halfpipe.

BOOTS AND BINDINGS

As with boards, your choice of boots and **bindings** is determined by the type of snowboarding you plan to do. Only **alpine** boards use hard boots, so if you prefer the idea of **freestyle** or **freeriding**, then soft boots are for you.

Soft boots and freestyle bindings

As you would expect, soft boots are more comfortable than hard boots. They are made of rubber and leather but are still strong enough to support your feet. Boots are connected to the board by freestyle bindings made of polycarbon or alloys, which hold the foot in place with straps tightened by clips.

Hard boots and plate-bindings

This system is only used with alpine boards for **carving** at high speeds. Metal bindings hold the boot on by the heel and toe and are fastened with a clip at the front. The boot itself is made of hard plastic and has several straps that can be tightened up.

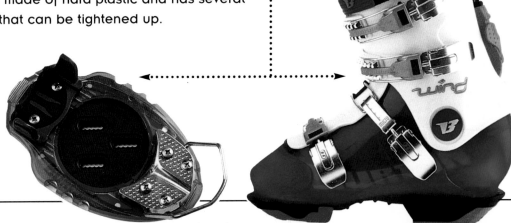

This is the latest development in boot technology—it takes the effort out of putting on your board. A special boot and binding combination allows you to lock into the bindings by just stepping onto the board. To step out, all you have to do is release a catch.

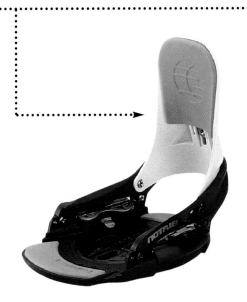

Choosing boots

Wear thick socks when trying on boots, and have both feet measured. Make sure your toes have room to wiggle, then leave the boots on for at least five minutes. Walk around in them to see how comfortable they are. If they hurt after five minutes, imagine how sore your feet will be after a whole day on the slopes. People usually need boots that are a size bigger than normal shoes. Don't fasten your boots or bindings too tightly—you don't want your fun on the slopes to be ruined by blisters.

This boy is choosing boots. Helped by an expert, he spends plenty of time trying them on and making sure the fit is just right.

THE RIGHT CLOTHES

For successful boarding you need the right clothing. It doesn't matter how good you are—if you are cold or uncomfortable you will not have any fun. Snowboarding clothing has been influenced by the loose-fitting clothes that skateboarders wear, so you can usually tell boarders apart from skiers just by what they are wearing.

Backpack
You will need something for carrying your essential equipment, such as sunscreen, food, and goggles.

Eyewear
It is always bright in the mountains, even on a cloudy day. Goggles or sunglasses improve visibility and protect your eyes from the glare of the snow. Eyewear should have UV protection to keep harmful ultraviolet rays from damaging your eyes.

Jacket
Jackets should be warm and waterproof, with a hood and zippered pockets. They should be made of a breathable material that allows sweat and heat to escape but keeps snow and rain out.

Gloves
Snowboarders' hands come into contact with the snow a lot. Whether you are pushing yourself up after a fall or trailing your hand on the ground as you **carve** stylish turns, you need a good pair of well-padded, waterproof gloves.

Snow pants
These should be waterproof and loose-fitting, to give you room to move. It helps if they are padded around the knees and backside.

Thick socks
There is nothing worse than cold feet to ruin a day on the slopes, so make sure you have thick thermal socks.

Helmet

Even the best snowboarders cannot help falling over every now and then, so it is important to protect yourself by wearing a helmet. Most body heat is lost through the head, so a warm hat is also a must.

TOP TIP

It may be cold up on the mountain, but the risk of sunburn is high, beause the sun's rays reflect up off the snow. Always use a high-protection sunscreen on your face and a total sun block on your lips.

Wrist guards

To reduce the risk of a break or sprain, wear wrist guards.

Knee and elbow pads

Protect your knees and elbows with special pads that can be worn under your clothing.

Clothing tips

Weather in the mountains is unpredictable—bright sunshine can quickly be replaced by blizzards. It is better to be too warm than too cold, so wear several layers on top. Thermal underwear provides an extra layer of warmth in cold conditions.

KEEPING FIT AND HEALTHY

It is important to prepare your body for any hard physical activity, so make sure you spend at least 15 minutes stretching thoroughly. Snowboarding uses the same muscles as many other sports, so the **warm-up** will be similar.

Warming up

Run in place for 10 minutes to get your blood pumping and your muscles warm.

Hips ···➤

Hold your arms out in front of you and rotate at the waist to one side, and then the other. Next, with your hands on your hips, lean over to one side and then the other. Finally, rotate your hips slowly to stretch your lower back.

Hamstring stretch ···································

With your legs apart, reach down and touch the ground between your toes. Then touch your left foot with both hands, come up, and do the same with the right foot.

Groin stretch

With your feet apart, turn to the right side and bend your right knee, keeping the left leg straight. Hold for 10 seconds, then do the same with the other leg.

Neck stretches

Turn your head to one side and hold it for 20 seconds, then turn it the other way and do the same. Next, bend your neck so your chin is on your chest. Hold it but do not bounce. Never bend your neck backwards, as this can damage it.

Cooling down

After a day of snowboarding, your muscles can get tight, increasing the risk of damage the next time you take to the slopes. You can prevent this by doing a cool-down. Jog in place or take a brisk walk, or repeat your warm-up stretches, but not for so long.

NUTRITION

 When you are doing any physical activity, your body needs lots of energy to function properly. The main source of energy comes from carbohydrates such as cereals, rice, bread, potatoes, and pasta.

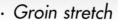 Give yourself some energy before boarding with a light meal that might consist of toast, oatmeal, or a small dish of pasta. Keep your fluid level up by drinking water regularly. Carry snack food with you on the slopes—bananas, raisins, or granola bars are ideal.

YOUR FIRST LESSON

What to expect

No one learns to snowboard without taking a few falls. In fact, for the first few hours you will be doing little else. But once you start to master the techniques, you will conquer the slopes in no time at all. Save yourself time and bruises by taking a few one-on-one lessons with a certified snowboard instructor.

Getting into the binding

When strapping in, always attach your **leash** first, so that the board does not run away. Then start by securing the front foot into the **binding**. It helps to sit on the ground and anchor the board by digging the **uphill edge** into the snow.

For comfort and performance, your boots must be flat and in the center of the bindings. Before you step in, brush away any snow from the bottoms of your boots or bindings. Fasten the ankle strap first—this will pull the boot into the binding. Then you can fasten the toe strap.

This is the best way to strap in. Sitting down, the rider digs the board into the snow to hold it steady, then fastens the bindings.

Basic riding stance

The basic snowboard **stance** is very similar to skateboarding or surfing. The rider stands sideways with one foot towards the front of the board and one towards the back. The rider is flexed at the knees and ankles, but not the hips, and the weight is balanced equally on both feet. The leading hand points forwards over the **nose** and the trailing hand points backwards over the **tail**.

Are you regular or goofy?

Regular means your left foot is forward and **goofy** means your right foot is forward. As a general rule, you should make your strongest foot your back foot. For example, if you kick a ball with your right foot, this should be your back foot.

This is the basic stance. The rider has his weight balanced evenly over both feet.

Balancing exercises

To get used to the strange sensation of being on a board, it helps to practice balancing. Start off by skating forwards on a flat slope with just your front foot in the binding. Then walk up the hill, using your free foot and the **toeside** edge of the board for grip. Once you have strapped in and are standing up, practice rocking onto the nose and onto the tail and **edging** the board on the toe and heel sides.

These riders both have different stances. The rider on the right is goofy (right foot forward) and the rider on the left is regular (left foot forward).

THE BASIC SKILLS

How to fall

Falling while snowboarding is completely different from falling while skiing. The **bindings** keep you attached to the board, so if the board gets stuck in the snow, you can be thrown in some strange directions.

It is important to know how to fall—you will be falling down a lot, and you need to minimize the risk of injury. Try to take the sting out of the fall by guarding your face with your forearms. Make your hands into fists to protect your wrists. If you can, keep a low center of gravity by bending your knees, so you have less distance to fall. Lift the snowboard clear of the snow when you fall.

As you fall, the instinctive reaction is to put out your hands to break the fall, which is why injuries to the wrist and fingers are common in snowboarding. To cut down the risk of a break or sprain, wear wrist guards. You can protect your knees and elbows with special pads that can be worn under your clothes. Don't forget your helmet!

This is the safest way to fall. The rider's fists are clenched to protect **the** fingers and wrists, and **the** forearms take the force of the fall.

Getting up

From a sitting position, bring the board as close to your body as possible. Grab the front of the board with one hand and use the other hand to push yourself up. For beginners it is easier to stand up when you are facing uphill. Grab your front knee, bring it into your chest, and roll around. Then push yourself up with your fists.

Stopping

To stop or slow down, turn the board sideways and scrape down the slope on your **uphill edge**. There are two ways to do this. If you are doing a **heelside** turn, dig the heelside edge in by lifting your toes. If you are doing a **toeside** turn, dig the toeside edge in by lifting your heels.

This rider shows the easiest way to get up. Facing the slope, he pushes himself up with his fists until he is standing up and ready to ride.

This boarder is stopping on the heelside edge. Using his outstretched arms for balance, he scrapes downhill with the board turned sideways until he comes to a stop.

TOP TIP

Experts recommend using hard boots for learning, as these are less flexible and make **edging** the board easier.

IMPORTANT TURNS

Before you can become a good boarder, you have
to master the basics.

A straight run
Once you are familiar with the feel of the board, make
a straight run down a gentle slope and allow the board
to come to a stop naturally.

····················· The side-slip

The **side-slip** is the boarder's way of braking. The
rider can side-slip when facing up or down the slope
by keeping the board at a right angle to the **fall
line**. On the **toeside** edge (facing uphill), lower
the heels to pick up speed and raise them to slow
down. On the **heelside** edge (facing downhill),
lower the toes for
speed and raise
them to slow down.

The falling leaf ·····································▶

This teaches you how to use your weight to turn the
board. As you side-slip, move your weight onto the right
foot to sweep downhill to the right, then onto the left foot to
change direction and sweep across to the left. This winding
left-to-right movement is like a leaf falling to the ground.
This can be done when facing either uphill or downhill.

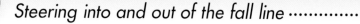

Steering into and out of the fall line

With your board pointing across the slope, gradually move your weight onto the front foot. Your board will start to turn downhill. To stop, increase pressure on the uphill edge and turn the board across the slope.

Traversing

To **traverse,** start with a side-slip, then use a weight transfer to guide the board across the slope on your **toe-edge**. Go back the other way on your **heel-edge**.

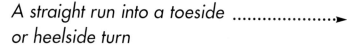

A straight run into a toeside or heelside turn

With your weight centered, run straight down the hill. Then transfer your weight to the front foot and raise your heel-edge by flexing or pushing your knees forward and rotating the board to make a toeside turn. To make a heelside turn, transfer the weight to the front foot and lift the toe-edge by raising your toes while keeping your knees flexed and sitting back slightly.

These turns can be linked. Between each turn, bring your weight back to the center and straighten your legs to stand up.

CATCHING A LIFT

Catching your first lift is not easy, but if you are going to come down you have to learn how to go up first.

Drag lifts
Drag lifts pull you up the slope on your board. These take the form of **button lifts** or **T-bars**, depending on which country you are in.

1. Take your back foot out of the **binding** and **skate** slowly up to the pick-up point.

2. Take the button or T-bar with your leading hand and put it between your legs.

3. Rest your back leg on the space between the front and rear binding. It helps to have a rubber **stomp pad** on the board to keep your boot from slipping off sideways.

4. Relax and keep your board flat as you are pulled uphill. Lean back a little to keep the lift from pulling you off balance.

5. Wait until you reach the very end of the lift, then pull the button or T-bar out from between your legs and gently release it. Glide to a halt before putting your boot back into the binding.

Catching a drag lift requires practice.

Chair lifts

1. Take your back foot out of the binding and skate slowly up to the take-off point. Turn and face the chair. As it approaches, put your hand out to keep it from knocking you over, and sit down.

2. As soon as you are under way, pull down the safety bar and rest your board on the footrest.

3. Lift the safety bar as you approach the top of the lift. Push off gently with your hand and, with your back foot on the stomp pad, glide to a halt before strapping back in.

Keep one foot free of the binding when getting on and off a chair lift.

SAFETY FIRST

- It is dangerous to fool around on lifts. If you try to jump or **slalom** as you are being pulled, you will fall off. This is embarrassing and you could slide back down the slope towards those coming up behind you. Always take your back foot out of the binding before catching a lift so you are less likely to hurt yourself if you fall.

- Don't rock the lift and always pull down the safety bar. Make sure your front foot is firmly strapped in before you get on, and watch out for other people as you get off.

CARING FOR YOUR EQUIPMENT

If you want to get the best out of your equipment you have to take care of it. Your board and **bindings** should be serviced professionally once a year, but there are also a few things you can do yourself to keep everything running smoothly. Caring for a board is not easy—it is best to ask an expert for help.

Waxing the board

Your board will travel faster if you wax it regularly.

1. Using an old iron (not a steam iron), melt some snowboard wax onto the board.

2. Spread it evenly with the iron.

3. Let the wax cool, then use a scraper to file off the excess, leaving just a thin layer.

WARNING: Never try this without the help of an adult.
NEVER use a steam iron.

Sharpening the edges

If the edges of the board are not sharp, it will affect your turning ability, so use a file to smooth out any rough places. Keep the file at a right angle to the edge and make sure you file along the whole length of the edge, or it can become uneven.

Bindings

Check your bindings every day when boarding. Wear and tear can loosen screws and damage straps—if these come undone as you are riding, it can be dangerous. Always carry a **mini driver** and a spare set of binding bolts just in case.

Boots

During a hard day's boarding, your boots will get wet. Water can penetrate through the stitching of the boots, so it helps to use a waterproofing spray. Boot linings should be taken out and dried, but don't put them directly on top of a radiator or heater, because drying them too quickly can damage the leather. If the boots are very wet, put newspaper inside to soak up moisture.

Clothing

Don't throw your clothes in a heap when you finish boarding for the day. There is nothing worse than going back out onto the slopes in damp, smelly gear— if you do you will not stay warm for long.

 TOP TIP

When you have finished riding for the season, don't just dump your board in the garage and forget about it. Boards rust and warp in damp conditions, so it's better to keep them in a warm place and cover them with a thick layer of wax.

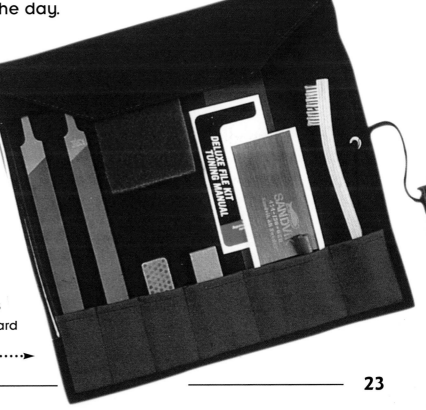

You'll need a selection of files to keep the edges of your board sharp and smooth.

SAFETY FIRST

The rules of the slopes

The basic rule of snowboarding is to have fun without putting yourself or others at risk.

- Stick to the marked trail at all times. The off-trail area is not patrolled or prepared—there may be dangerous trees, rocks, avalanches, or even **crevasses** lying in wait for the unsuspecting boarder.

- Never attempt anything you are not ready for. As you improve you will become more adventurous, but if you want to jump, build up to it slowly. Never jump off anything unless you know there is a safe landing on the other side.

Warning signs are there for a reason—don't ignore them! This sign tells riders that the trail ahead is closed. Going beyond the rope means putting yourself at risk.

- Keep your distance from other skiers and boarders. Sometimes they change direction unexpectedly, and if you are too close you will not have time to avoid them. Remember that the rider in front always has priority.

- Before you turn, take a quick look up the slope to make sure you will not cross the path of anyone coming down. Never stop suddenly without checking whether anyone is behind you, and always stop in an area where people coming from behind will be able to see you. If you want to rest, make sure you stop on the edge of the trail.

- Slow down early as you approach the line for the lift. If you try to stop at the last minute and make a mistake, you could end up getting hurt or hurting others. Don't cut into lift lines—this is one of the most annoying things any skier or boarder can do.

- Don't go too fast in beginners' areas. Even if you think that you are in control, others may not be.

- Keep your **lift pass** safe. If you lose it, you will have to pay for another one. Make sure you know when the lifts close. If you try to catch a last run around closing time you could find yourself stranded on the mountain.

Be alert as you approach a lift line. Skiers and boarders will often be coming from different directions, so slow down well in advance.

SNOWBOARDING EVENTS

There are a number of snowboarding contests that give the stars a chance to shine. Some are part of a world tour and others are just exhibition events, but there are often big prizes at stake. Competitions are not just confined to ski resorts—a few take place in specially created arenas in the middle of cities that hardly ever see snow.

Halfpipe

The tricks of the **halfpipe** evolved from skateboarding and surfing. Riders take turns going down the pipe, crossing from one wall to the other and doing jumps and spins off each side. A panel of judges chooses the winner.

Boardercross

In a **boardercross** event, groups of four to six riders race downhill against each other over a course of bumps, gates, jumps, and banked turns. The competition is run in heats and the best riders go head-to-head in a grand final. Physical contact between riders is allowed, but they are not allowed to push or shove with their shoulders.

Canadian Ross Rebagliati took the gold in the giant **slalom** at the 1998 winter Olympics. His tight clothing and **alpine** board gave him extra speed.

Slalom

In giant slalom, riders take turns racing down a course of 25 gates, each placed about 65 feet (20 meters) apart. The winner is the rider who clocks the fastest time. There is also a dual slalom event, in which two riders race side by side down parallel courses. The best time over two runs wins.

MUSIC

 Music is a very important part of the snowboarding scene—you will always hear tunes blasting out of the speakers at competitions. Boarders' favorites include dance music, hip-hop, and drum and bass.

Other events

In **slope style** contests, competitors ride over a series of different jumps and are judged on the quality of their tricks and maneuvers. There are also **quarterpipe** contests, where riders use just one curved wall for jumps rather than two. But perhaps the most daring of all are the **big air** contests. Riders take turns launching themselves off a big jump and are judged for the style of their trick.

A fearless rider spins high above the ground in a big air contest. Top boarders spend hours practicing in order to impress the judges with the most spectacular trick.

THE INTERNATIONAL SCENE

Everyone has their favorite boarder, but here are some of the top riders currently setting their sport ablaze.

Marguerite Cossettini (Australia)

Marguerite became the first women's **boardercross** world champion in 1997 and won the title again the following year. She has been boarding since 1988 and is the survivor of two avalanches.

Sasha Ryzy (Australia)

A boardercross and **big air** expert, Sasha spends half the year racing in Australia and New Zealand and the other half competing in Canada, Europe, Japan, and the United States.

Nicola Thost (Germany)

Nicola started off as a skier but crossed over to boarding. It paid off when she became junior World Champion, then won the **halfpipe** gold medal at the 1998 Winter Olympics.

Terje Haakonsen (Norway)

Freestyle master Terje has dominated the competition for years and consistently jumps almost 9 feet (2.7 meters) out of the halfpipe. He is so good that he once started a **slalom** course riding **fakie** (backwards) and still won.

Daniel Franck (Norway)

Daniel is one of the few riders to beat Terje Haakonsen in a halfpipe competition. He also won a silver medal at Nagano in 1988.

Jamie Lynn (USA)

Jamie started off riding mountain bikes and skateboarding, but became one of the best boarders in the world. He is also a talented artist and surfer.

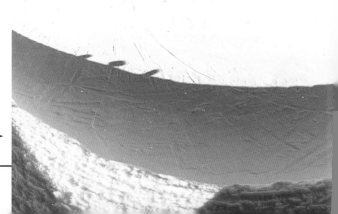

Melanie Leando shows the skills that made her the British halfpipe champion in 1998. She hopes to win a medal at the next Winter Olympics. ·····················➤

Jamie Phillp is one of the few British boarders with experience on the world circuit. He is a halfpipe specialist and has already starred in several snowboard action videos.

Michelle Taggart (USA)

As world halfpipe champion for four years in a row, Michelle has become a legend in the snowboarding world.

Ross Powers (USA)

Ross won a bronze medal in the halfpipe at the Winter Olympics in Nagano in 1998.

Lesley McKenna and Melanie Leando (UK)

Lesley and Melanie are Britain's top female boarders. They started the British Women's Snowboarding Team, and they are role models for women boarders everywhere.

Extreme events

There are some riders out there who will go to any length to test their limits. The craziest of all extreme contests is the King of the Hill in Alaska. This four-day event involves a freestyle course of big jumps, a very tricky slalom and an extreme descent where the first rider to reach the bottom wins.

WARNING: This type of riding is extremely dangerous— even the best riders get hurt doing it.

Winter Olympics

Snowboarding showed how far it had come when it was chosen to become an Olympic medal event in 1998. At Nagano, Japan, riders competed for medals in slalom and halfpipe events.

GLOSSARY

alpine   type of snowboarding done in hard boots that involves fast carving turns

big air   contest in which boarders jump off a ramp and perform tricks before landing

bindings   devices used to attach the rider's feet to the board

boardercross   downhill event where boarders race side-by-side over a course of bumps and gates

button lift   drag lift with a button-shaped plate that the boarder puts between his or her legs to catch a lift up the mountain

carve   to turn the board on its edge without sliding

crevasse   gap in the mountainside

drag lift   machine that pulls riders up the mountain on their boards

edging   digging the edge of the board into the snow to turn, slow down, or stop

fakie   riding backwards

fall line   imaginary line pointing straight down the hill

freeriding   snowboarding on all types of terrain for fun

freestyle   type of snowboarding involving tricks and jumps

goofy   riding with the right foot forward

halfpipe   U-shaped trench on a downward slope used for freestyle snowboarding

heel-edge/heelside   side of the board where the heels rest

leash   safety device used to attach the board to the front foot, so that it does not get away

lift pass   pass that skiers and boarders pay for to use the lifts

mini driver   small screwdriver used to make adjustments to bindings

nose   front tip of the snowboard

P-tex   clear material that makes up the flat running surface of the snowboard

plate-binding   flat plate used to connect hard boots to an alpine board

quarterpipe   similar to a halfpipe but using just one curved wall for jumps rather than two

regular   riding with the left foot forward

side-slip   moving downhill with the board facing directly across the slope and the boarder using the uphill edge to control speed

skating   propelling the board along on flat terrain with the back foot free and the front foot in the binding

ski lift   device used to transport boarders and skiers up the mountain

slalom   snowboarding event involving zigzagging down a course of gates

slope style   contest in which riders go off different jumps and are judged on their tricks

stance   position of the feet on the snowboard

step-in binding   catch system for attaching boot to board by just stepping onto the board

stomp pad   non-slip pad attached to the board between the bindings to stop the rear foot from slipping when getting on and off lifts

T-bar   T-shaped drag lift that pulls the rider up the slope

tail   rear tip of the snowboard

toe-edge/toeside   edge of the snowboard where the toes rest

traversing   riding the board across the slope on the toeside or heelside edge

twin-tip   board with an identically-shaped nose and tail, used for freestyling

uphill edge   edge of the board that is highest up the slope as the rider is traversing

warm-up   exercises to prepare the body for boarding

....

A snowboarder's terms

The vocabulary of snowboarding is weird and wonderful. Here are a few bizarre words and phrases that you might hear on the slopes.

bail   to fall over

boost   to catch air off a jump

burger flip, flying squirrel air, roast

beef air, Swiss cheese air   types of snowboard tricks

fat air   big air

grommet   a dedicated, young snowboarder

sick   very good

stoked   very excited

30

USEFUL ADDRESSES

Snowboarding has become so popular that you can find local clubs almost anywhere there are ski slopes. There are enthusiasts even in places where it never snows! Your local ski shop is a good place to find out about clubs and competitions. Here are addresses for some of the national and international snowboarding organizations. They run most of the larger competitions and are good sources of information on boarding events.

U.S. Ski and Snowboard Association
P.O. Box 100
Park City, UT 84060
435-649-9090

USA Snowboard Association
P.O. Box 3927
Truckee, CA 96160
530-587-6656

International Snowboard Federation (ISF)
Pradlerstrasse 21
A6020 Innsbruck
Austria

MORE BOOKS TO READ

Armentrout, David. *Snowboarding.* Vero Beach, Fla.: The Rourke Book Company, Inc., 1997.

Iguchi, Bryan. *The Young Snowboarder: A Young Enthusiast's Guide to Snowboarding.* New York: DK Publishing, 1997.

Lund, Bill, and Pat Ryan. *Extreme Snowboarding.* Danbury, Conn.: Children's Press, 1997.

Lurie, Jon. *Fundamental Snowboarding.* Minneapolis: The Lerner Publishing Group, 1996.

McKenna, Lesley. *Fantastic Book of Snowboarding.* Brookfield, Conn.: Millbrook Press, 1998.

INDEX

$22.79

DATE			